Dr. PP Radhakrishnan

THE CRAVING HEARTS

Rtn. Dr. PP Radhakrishnan

NOTION PRESS

NOTION PRESS

India. Singapore. Malaysia.

This book has been published with all reasonable efforts taken to make the material error-free after the consent of the author. No part of this book shall be used, reproduced in any manner whatsoever without written permission from the author, except in the case of brief quotations embodied in critical articles and reviews.

The Author of this book is solely responsible and liable for its content including but not limited to the views, representations, descriptions, statements, information, opinions and references ["Content"]. The Content of this book shall not constitute or be construed or deemed to reflect the opinion or expression of the Publisher or Editor. Neither the Publisher nor Editor endorse or approve the Content of this book or guarantee the reliability, accuracy or completeness of the Content published herein and do not make any representations or warranties of any kind, express or implied, including but not limited to the implied warranties of merchantability, fitness for a particular purpose. The Publisher and Editor shall not be liable whatsoever for any errors, omissions, whether such errors or omissions result from negligence, accident, or any other cause or claims for loss or damages of any kind, including without limitation, indirect or consequential loss or damage arising out of use, inability to use, or about the reliability, accuracy or sufficiency of the information contained in this book.

Dedicated to

all Craving Hearts.

.

"I AM A CITIZEN, NOT OF
ATHENS OR GREECE BUT
OF THE WORLD"

SOCRATES

Contents

Preface 7

I TWO LETTERS 9

II   THE FIRST LOVE 33

III THE INNOCUOUS 49

IV   THE SPINSTER 60

V. VIRTUOUS WOMEN 76

STORY GISTS............................92

REVIEWS OF OTHER BOOKS 102

Preface

Here I am trotting out my 6th book 'The Craving Hearts' which is an agglomeration of five short love stories. They all expose the multifarious nature of love, profound attachments, emotions, intimacies etc. between men and women both married as well as single. The cravings of their hearts are distinct and will appear even sacrosanct. I hope you will enjoy reading them.

My earlier books 'Story of Ravikumar' '7 Stories' 'Col. Sandeep' 'The Impre - ssions' and 'Her Confessions' seem to have been well received. This factor inspired me to pen a new thought.

I wish to express my deep gratitude to the readers, well-wishers and the publishers for their unfeigned support and encouragement.

Dr. P P Radhakrishnan

20th May 2024

I TWO LETTERS

Sub Lieutenant (Sub Lt.) Anish enrolled for MA English Literature programme of prestigious Sri Venkateswara University along with his sister Reena. He was posted at Indian Naval Ship (INS) 'Darshak' in Bombay (Mumbai); but the ship just got moved to the dry dock for a long refit which was to take at least a year or perhaps more. Naturally there wasn't much work except the officer-on-duty which occurred once in three days on rotation basis; all other days were casual summer routine and everyone got free by 1.30 noon.

The ship had minimum strength of men and officers; One Lt. Cdr. as the ship's captain, a Lt. rank officer as Chief Executive Officer and three Sub Lts., two chief petty officers, five petty officers and around 35 others so as to take care of the routine work and general upkeep of the ship's upper and lower decks.

Anish straight away on completing his B.Sc with physics and mathematics got enrolled as a Naval Officer after an initial training of some six months. His sister Reena signed up for the English literature programme of S V University, as her father did not want her to do the PG course staying in far distant hostel and this course did not demand a full time college class room attendance except that they needed to join for final examinations at the 2nd year end. Candidates were allowed to do home studies by picking up one of the senior empaneled professors as their Guide cum Mentor who would ensure the students complied with all the prescribed university guidelines, norms, regulations, contact sessions and so on.

Anish's sister somehow came to know about this and joined for two years PG programme and got an eminent and renowned professor – Prof. KKR Rao, who was a highly respected and reputed scholar with some nine PG degrees from different universities. It was Reena who persuaded her brother Anish to take up this course so that they could do their exams by travelling and staying together at the end of two years in one stretch.

Prof. Rao promptly dispatched study notes together with his excellent elaborate detailed notes by post in a consistent fashion as the course necessitated lots of reading and writing. Anyway, both Sub.Lt. Anish and his sister Reena found the Programme very riveting.

Exams were in the month of May and Anish took his annual leave and arrived home well in advance. Both of them studied for long hours everyday; while Reena had been reading her notes on daily basis, that was not the case with Anish who read too little or nil on regular basis while he was on board ship, but at home he started reading for sixteen hours daily. Both proceeded for examinations by train which was a 12-hours journey.

Prof. Rao had already done their boarding and lodging arrangements at Balaji Hotel and the students were asked to be there 5-days prior to the exams, as he wanted to take almost non-stop classes during that period.

All male students were asked to look for their own arrangements at the beginning itself. The entire rooms on the hotel's first floor were reserved for the students on twin sharing basis. The only male who was put up there was Anish along with his sister Reena; other 5 - Rooms were allotted to ladies, all doing MA English Literature.

Prof. KKR Rao showed up by 11.45 in the morning, handed over keys to all students of the respective rooms and announced that the entire floor was strictly meant for women and the only exception he made was for Reena's brother, a Naval officer. Dr. Rao added that one occupant, Devi was an Air Force Officer's wife and Rajeshwari, a Jr.college lecturer of a women's college in Trichy, who was an MA History with MPhil and perusing her PG in literature. He then asked everybody to be present fora brief self-introduction. Later Dr. Rao spoke about himself for a minute and a half, got on to some brief information about Tirupati, the university and food available in the hotel, all of course pure vegetarian. He told us about the examination schedule, the transport facility to the examination center in the university main building. He informed us that in each paper there would be 6-8 questions and only 4 needed to be answered in three hours. But the subject being literature, the students were required to write extensively, taking several pages and speed in writing was a must, he highlighted.

The first year and second year put together there were altogether 8-papers in 8-days and the examination timing was 2pm to 5 pm. Month being May, heat was at its peak and they were told to drink lots of water. Professor announced that he would be back for lecture in the afternoon which would be 3 to 7 or beyond and would go through important probable questions.

He suggested that all students to make it a point to visit the Tirupati Balaji Temple and receive the divine blessings before departing Tirupati on culmination of examinations. He then narrated briefly about the temple, which is situated in the hills of Tirumala and dedicated to Lord Venkateswara, a form of Vishnu, who is believed to have appeared to rescue the mankind from trials and turmoil of Kali Yuga. Hence, the place has also got the name Kaliyuga Vaikuntha and the deity here is referred to as Kaliyuga Prathyaksha Daivam. The temple is also known by other names like Tirumala Temple, Tirupati Temple and Tirupati Balaji Temple. Venkateswara is known by many other names: Balaji, Govinda, and Srinivasa. The temple is run by Tirumala Tirupati Devasthanams (TTD). The temple is one of the Pancha Kshethram, where Mahalakshmi was born as Bhargavi - the daughter of Maharishi Bhrigu. The temple was built by Thondaman king and reformed periodically by Cholas, Pandyas and Vijaynagar rulers. This is built in Indian architecture and is believed to have been done over a period of time beginning from 300 CE. There are many legends linked to the manifestation of the deity in Tirumala. As per one, the temple has a murti of Venkateswara and believed that this will remain there for the entire span of the present Kali Yuga.

The exams were to commence after 4 days and added that he would take classes 10 hours daily. He thanked, wished all and departed saying he would meet them next day at 10 in the morning. The lobby space was to be used for lecture purpose and as such every student needed to bring 2 chairs that were kept in every room. He suggested that the time to go down and take breakfast was 8.30, lunch 12.30, evening tea and snacks at 5 and dinner would be at 8.00 pm. During then, the hotel would try to seat them cozily at a particular space to enable them to sit together and chit chat for a while before the crowd barged in.

It was at the introduction time that all met each other, and Sub. Lt. Anish fortuitously took a special note of the extremely enchanting Devi. She was tall, slim but healthy with long nose and had awesome flowing hair. She had a shining face and her eyes were blue and beautiful. The blue chiffon sari robed her body with a light blue coloured blouse which coordinated with her well curved body. For a moment he thought that she was an angel and her posture was too dignified and illuminating. Anish could not recall of seeing someone like that anywhere earlier. The earrings, eye lashes, the sleek gold chain she wore enhanced her exquisiteness. For a moment he thought the creator must have taken outright care and time on her. While everybody there looked at her delightfully as an epitome of beauty, Devi noted Anish's slightly protracted look, which perhaps she rejoiced entirely.

Slowly and steadily they became friends, specially at the dining table, while mostly all others were fully engrossed in confabulating the works of Shakespeare, Francis Bacon, Wordsworth, Charles Dickens, Shelly, George Bernard Shaw and such others.

Rajeshwari, the intelligent Jr. lecturer started visiting Anish's room under the guise of talking or sharing most expected questions and things like that mainly with Reena. She was fluent in English and was fond of talking to Anish as well. She hardly spoke with anybody else. Anish sensed she was trying to impress him; all other excuses were mere alibis.

Anish had an intuitive mind; by and large his thoughts, assumptions and hunch fell right. However, when he sounded this to his sister, she said that he was reading others' minds rather too far and Rajeshwari was exceptionally good in studies, knowledgeable and a diligent woman. But Anish told her that he would prove to be right and Reena would have to wait for a while. The lecturer enquired about their eating habits, likes, dislikes, special interests, belief system, their parents and other people at home etc. As for her, she has just her parents, grandparents and the only younger brother who was doing engineering. She added that though she was a staunch vegetarian, she wouldn't mind eating non-veg if after marriage, her husband liked non-veg, and mentioned most of the people in Defense services ate and relished non-vegetarian food.

The next day, Prof. Rao reached the first floor 5 minutes before time and all of them came out with their chairs and sat swiftly. Professor greeted everyone post haste and commenced the session.

The hotel area and the floor was quiet most of the time which was apt for focused reading and studies. But there were a few short comings; for instance, though they were all double rooms, they were not good enough to put two single cots on either side, one table and two small wooden chairs in between with an extra table fan.

In effect it was a lodge, and washrooms were only at one end of the lobby and they were close to the room where Anish and Reena were put up. Everybody kept their doors opened because of the torrid heat and everyone who walked to the washroom would peep into their room. While Anish in a way enjoyed each time Devi walked through, Rajeshwari most of the time looked and walked into the room under one pretext or the other for she was only bent upon impressing Anish. Devi and others assembled or indulged in small talk only while eating.For exams, mostly they all went more or less at the same time and returned after the exams too in that manner.

On the last day of the exams though everybody planned to visit the Balaji Temple,Devi, her roommate, Anish and his sister were together as they had to travel by the same night train, while others were leaving by Bus to their relatively closer destinations. But they all got in at the temple by 5.15 evening or so before the crowd erupted and all of them could have a closer vision of the Lord.

Incidentally, the Chief Priest was a former student of their Professor K. K. R. Rao and they were allowed a little longer time there; he had a great admiration for Rao and treated them well. As Devi was very close to Anish, he offered special Prasad and Blessings to those two misperceiving them as couple;both Devi and Anish smiled.

They then walked around the temple and returned to the town, took some tea and got refreshed themselves. A little later they had dinner and left to catch the 10pm train which was fine for all the four. Devi's roommate's station was to come first which would touch by early morning 3.30, Devi was to get down at Coimbatore by 5.30. It was a few hours more for

Anish and his sister Reena to alight. While Devi collected the residence address from Anish, Rajeshwari took his ship address from Reena earlier.

The train was jam-packed but somehow four of them got in and laid their bags at the middle of the compartment entrance space close to the washroom side and sat down together. Anyway, there after hardly any room was left for anyone to get in or move even an inch in that general compartment, and others who positioned closed to either side of compartment also kept the doors closed. They spread newspapers on their captured area and then Reena took out and spread a bed sheet and managed to lie down to sleep for a while as to make up part of their lost sleep, for by and large they were all reading up to midnight, waking up at 4 a.m., and perhaps had forty winks after lunch before stepping out for exams.

It so happened that they slept – Anish, Devi Reena and Devi's roommate,which she suggested as she would be the first to get down, and everyone used their bags in lieu of pillows and also that as a matter of safety. Anish took out a long cotton sheet from the bag to cover his body and protect from the dust and so on,especially while people walked to the washroom. Though they spoke for a few minutes, they could not escape from falling asleep in a short time. As the train moved, noise got assuaged and almost all others too went to sleep as they could not resist it any further. All lights were put off except the small blue night lamps here or there.

The wind outside became a bit cool which penetrated through the door's rusty grills, the moon light played the game of touching them and then hiding between the tree leaves outside; Devi was feeling cold which Anish sensed, impetuously extended his cotton sheet which he had on his body and she gladly snatched it and also moved near to him to facilitate sharing or to cover him well. Slowly and steadily all fell asleep.But Anish and Devi did not or could not sleep; they were awake and getting more familiar in that darkness. Their thoughts were getting narrowed and they gleefully moved closer; both put their arms around on each other spoke nothing but heard well. It appeared the cotton sheet was too wide and half of it would have sufficed. The two bodies and minds slowly got enwrapped in a part of that cloth; they felt no cold, heard no sound, saw no light. They were completely lost in themselves each caring, covering and loving the other.They just perdured as one and their only wish was the night to linger lengthier.

When the halt station of Devi's roommates approached, she precipitously got up, uttered bye and stepped out. The dawn was slowly breaking; it was almost time to reach Coimbatore station where Devi had to disembark and all of them briskly got up. At the station Anish accompanied Devi, helped to hold the bag while Reena stood at the door side to bid farewell. Anish told Reena he would go with her up to the waiting room as there was some 5 minutes halt. When the train whistled, they sobbed, shook hands, said bye and muttered to each other that they would meet again. She quickly took down his home address.

After two hours the train reached their station, they hired a cab and went home. Anish had another four days to go for going back to Mumbai. On the third day he received the letter from Devi which she scribbled on reaching home. It was a very short letter wishing him well and saying she enjoyed the stay at Tirupati and the opportunity of seeing and knowing him.

Then she added that the train journey was most enjoyable, and she would treasure and remember that perennially. She then wrote" I wish, pray, hope and trust to meet you again sometime, my heart craves for you."Anish perused the letter several times, kept closed to his chest for a while but did not show it to his sister.

On the fifth day after reaching on board ship Sub Lt. Anish received a registered letter from Rajeshwari which ran to several pages, describing how much she loved him from the first sight itself and could not think of a life without him. She said she had informed this matter to all her family members learned how to make omelets and would soon be a non-vegetarian after marriage with him and she would make him very comfortable; would respect all his family members and all his likes and choices would be her's as well. He put all those papers in to a cover and posted to his sister Reena, putting a small script to Reena "in future you better trust his intuitions".On the outer cover Anish scribbled "much ado about nothing".

****

II   THE FIRST LOVE

Vinay was visiting Kerala after a gap of four years,his last visit was in September 2019 just for two days. The trip was for the junior college Alumni, first get together fest at the college premises after a gap of some 5 decades. The alumni itself was formed 3 months ago – thanks to the initiatives taken by some of the old college classmates.

The invitation came just at the right time when he was intermittently thinking about his favorite two lecturers of that time, and some of his most first loved faces.

One, and that was the first, when he was doing his 10th std. and her name was Mallika. They met and interacted at the time of final examinations and that continued for about two years. They started meeting more often, spent lots of time together and also exchanged some love letters. Eventually they liked each other so much and he even said he would marry her in the future, once studies got over and secured a job. However, that was not to be. He left for studies to Mumbai, and got into the job and things like that. The circumstances changed for Vinay but once through some sources he came to know that since they both reached 24 years of age she wanted to know from him if he would marry her. Vinay did not respond then; later she got married to someone after a gap of 2-3 years. So he wanted to meet her once, confess to her and ask forgiveness. Vinay thought and believed that he owed it to her.

He conveyed this to his close friend and sought to gather her where abouts or phone contacts, but he couldn't manage that as the time was to short but promised to collect that in a month time or so.

As for the other, the second love Lakshmi, he could gather her phone number, but she was living a little far away he could not go and see but spoke over the phone for a while and said he would see her next time.

So, Vinay decided to do these two things during this four days stays in Kerala, though the primary purpose was to attend the wedding of a close relative. He planned to go and meet them one after another after the wedding. Mallika was at 'Triur' – that was three hours train journey from Cochin and Lakshmi was put up near 'Trissur'. As soon as he got in to the train, Vinay started thinking about Mallika of those days; her husband passed away some 3 years ago and her only son was a small time politician – not working or getting paid. How does Mallika look like now? She was very beautiful then but that was 50 years ago! How would she react when she sees him or recalls old days?. A thousand thoughts came to his mind. He phoned his friend and luckily got her cell number but added that he heard from one of her relatives that she was extremely ill with diabetes, bed ridden at home, not able to sleep, listen or comprehend things and she was under the constant care of his 38 years old unmarried son. This news put down Vinay very badly, but he prayed for the best, and thought he would be able to meet and speak to her for some time. As the train reached, he hired a cab and set straight to her place, making enquiry on the way several times, as she lived in the interiors and he was not very familiar with those roads and by-lanes. Finally someone guided saying the second house at end of lane towards left side with closed gate was the house of Mallika teacher who later retired as the panchayat secretary, couple of years ago.

Vinay got out of the taxi at the gate of the house, but the gate appeared locked. It looked as if it was a locked house and that was a ground floor plus one house. The Maruti light blue car was covered by the dust fully and there was no indication that anyone stayed there for a long time. However, when he continuously pressed the bell at the gate, a man appeared slowly by opening one side of the door and paced to the gate. He asked him to remain in the small veranda and got back with glass of water. Vinay introduced himself saying he had come to see Mallika teacher and they wrote 10th std. examination together and then knew each other well. He said his mother was extremely diabetic, ill and was in the hospital for many days and got discharged just two days ago; also she was not able to speak or recognize anyone and was under his constant care.

Vinay insisted that he had travelled all the way from Mumbai to meet her after a gap of 5 decades and she would indeed recognize. He asked him to sit and wait so that he would try and wake her up; and it was also the time for her to eat something. So he went in to bring her to the dining table. After some 15 minutes he asked him to go inside where she was seated. He saw a thin, short skeleton like body wrapped in a short sari. He spoke about their travelling towards the S.S.L.C. exams and afew other things. She just stared through her half opened tired eyes, absolutely blank and she could not figure out or follow anything. His son started helping her with rice porridge water with a spoon which poured out through both sides of her partially opened mouth. Her loose blouse and the fallen sari had given way for the flat skinny upper body as if 'that is all what I am now left with'. She did not speak a single word.

Vinay went on talking slowly and repeatedly many old things to help her recollect him, but nothing of that sort happened. Almost half an hour passed – she was feeling sleepy. Vinay stood up, slowly kept his hands on her head and dried forehead and said he would be leaving. Then he noticed two tiny waterdrops slowly rolling down her wrinkled cheekson to his palm; tears rolled down from his eyes too. He sobbed, kept his right palm on her head once again; the tears were getting mixed up and touching the floor. He whispered bye and left.

After a few hours he boarded another train to visit his second love Lakshmi which occurred in his early 20s and she was a few years younger. Perhaps he did not even know for sure that she had any such intense feelings towards him. Though during his earlier visit he spoke with her on phone but not much, here too the separation was more than four decades but he had an extreme craving to see her before he died. And he always believed this meeting too would happen. His instinct, intuition told him that would happen, however late that could be.

Lakshmi was hardly eighteen years when he met her first, she was in 2nd year Dentistry and happened to be at her home not far from his home. Vinay went to her house to meet her parents who were friendly with his family members. Vinay was on a short leave from Mumbai. He had only his schooling at his home town and then went out for further studies to Mumbai while he was a teenager. She might have been some ten years or so then. Vinay had seen her during those days but did not notice or ever spoken with her.

His plan was actually to spent about 20-30 minutes at her placeas he had to visit a few more houses too before he left for Mumbai. But it took a different turn altogether, he spent two hours there talking with Lakshmi and occasionally to her mother. Lakshmi was very beautiful and almost looked like a mermaid; she was slim, tall with long curly hair, long nose and wide blue eyes. She had beautiful cheeks, well shaped lips and elegant voice; she could sing well and infact she sung couple of songs for him which he listened and admired repeatedly. She too was very impressed with him for his charming personality and his deep knowledge on variety of subjects. They liked each other so well, in other way they had good chemistry. Finally, when he said bye, she followed him up to the gate and said "lets meet again, you are fantastic. Day after tomorrow I will return to the hostel and we would meet only in the next year when you come". She held his warm hand, smiled beautifully and said "good night". The moon was glaring at them, though partially covered by the tall mango tree branch leaves at the gate.

On the following day, he visited her home a bit early and spent lots of time chatting on a variety of things. They sat close, ate snacks and sipped coffee together. Then touched, kissed quite a few times, held each other's hands together. Time fleeted and while leaving he said "I wish to marry you, once your study is over; I will pray God to move the years fast". She said taking a deep breath "I am yours and shall wait". The moon witnessed and shed its light making them feel that it is just above the mango tree.

Unfortunately in the next year when Vinay came home she was on a college arranged study tour and in the year that followed he could not manage leave owing to his work exigency and also the pre promotional training etc. By the time he came on leave later, she got married to a distant cousin of her'sand had to quickly go with him overseas, where he worked. His parents proposed and immediately his parents approved and perhaps she could not help. May be the time and circumstances were such. Vinay had no occasion to meet her later in those for decades, but craved to see heronce some time and She is now undergoing treatment in the hospital. She had been suffering from substantial memory loss which occurred due to a fall 3 months ago. One of her relatives informed that she was hardly able to speak or recognize anyone ever since and as per the Doctors, it would take considerable time and treatment in the hospital; her husband stayed there with her. Vinay hoped and believed that she would recognize him though the gap has been too long.

Vinay reached the hospital in the evening visit hours and sister there conveyed to her husband who was inside the room with her. After sometime he came out but vinay had never met him earlier. Vinay told him that his wife knew him quite well being his neighbour in the early days but not seen later. He asked Vinay to wait outside, so that he would check if she was awake but cautioned whether she would be able to remember anything or him. After sometime he opened the door and invited him to the special large room where he also stayed all the time; the room had an extra bed too with a side table and chair.

Vinay called out his name two three times, and started saying many things of the past days, as suggested by her husband to help recognize him, if at all. To his utter dismay, she slowly opened her eyes and looked at him. Then he kept his palm on her forehead and asked "could you recognize me; I had come all the way from Mumbai to see you". She Slowly whispered 'yes', smiled and signalled him to sit on the side of the bed which was a huge surprise for her husband and the nurse who instantly ran out to call the Doctor. Vinay kept saying few instances of those days sitting on the side of the bed. Then he slowly put his fingers on her hair and head. Tears rolled down her cheeks but she smiled. Vinay could not control his tears- a few drops came out of his eyes as well which got conjoined hers'. Visiting time was getting over and he signaled bye and left. Her husband thanked him profusely for it was almost a miracle and never happened anytime in three months despite repeated efforts by the Doctors. The Doctor was hugely surprised and stated, "the worst is over, and the situation would certainly improve quickly from now".

****

III THE INNOCUOUS

Hari joined a medium size manufacturing company as 'Special Executive' to the whole time Director. The office was in south Mumbai, in close proximity to Bombay Hospital and this was his second job. He did his post-graduation, worked for about three years with the previous company. He was smart, tall, handsome, and impressive with excellent communication skills. He just turned 25 years of age. The Director told him to use his car to travel as he was living close to Worli and to bill the car running expenses on reimbursement basis to the company. Salary was good, working five and half day a week which included the factory visit on Wednesday.

He was to join on the first of July, but it rained heavily that day, hence he reach head office very late. He walked to the Director's cabin and informed him he would resume office next day a she didn't want to join the first day office late,the Director acceded to his request. On the following day he came by 9 as the office timings were from 9:30 to 5:30 with half an hour lunch break. On all Saturdays, the office was only upto 1:30.

Hari was introduced to everyone and the Executive secretary Marina took him to his secretary-cum-Accounts Assistant Jayawanti. That cabin had a long table, a few chairs, phone, intercom, shelves, file cabinets. Air conditioners were installed only in the Director's cabin, Executive Secretary's small cabin and in Hari's cabin.

There were other two halls – one small and the other big. In the smaller one, sat the Sales cum office Manager Kannubhai, Accountant Purohit, stenotypist Karkera and in the bigger one there were sales teams consisting of two ladies and one gentleman, three office peons and Leena, the receptionist cum telephone operators at at the entrance. The Director usually reached the office around noon as he played Golf in the morning and then spent time at the Race course as he loved betting which was known to all.

In variably his mood on arrival at the office depended on the day's game. He raised his voice, had frowning face and shouted at staff but never ever at his Executive secretary Marina or Jayawanti; as he entered his cabin, the senior most office peon Ganjubhai – who had been there for more than 40 years went to him with a big tender coconut, large glass and a straw. Later he served him the coconut malai and some cookies. By 2 o'clock he often left, took lunch with his friends or clients in any top hotel and returned around 5 p.m. or still late. He dictated a lot of lengthy letters to his secretary Marina.

Hari's secretary and cabin mate Jayawanti was an M.Com first class, smart, tall, slim, very attractive and good looking. She kept her straight hair with middle partition which fell neatly to her shoulder level. She had long nose, beautiful shining eyes and looked classy, carried herself well and always walked straight. She smiled splendiferously and spoke in very gentle voice. She had long hands and limbs, mostly she wore sari or kurta pajama. All dresses suited her and her intermittent blinking of her eyes had an inexplicable charm. She worked neatly, typed well without mistakes and kept all records and documents neatly and in order.

The very first day itself she took special care of him, opened his briefcase took out his small tiffin box and kept near to her's. She got him coffee or tea as he needed, served his lunch and kept her's in plates with spoons. She kept a little of her lunch in his plate after asking and kept a little of her's for him, after ensuring food was vegetarian. She was a Jain, married to a financial consultant, travelled by train as she lived in a western suburbs close to Malad railway station. She was 26 years old, got married 5 years ago and had no child yet.

He liked the way she took care of him leaving no chance for any concern or discomfort to him. Then the first Saturday came after four days, that was 5th July and she asked him if she could join him in the car and spend some time taking a round in that part of the city and also view some of the major gardens there. She sat with him and drove to Nariman Point, Marine Drive,Colaba and Flora Fountain. They took some fruit juices, sat along the beach and she suggested to spend some time in the garden close to Charni Road railway station. The garden was exquisite with lots of plants and trees though very few sat there; then it rained quite a lot and both sat on a broad garden bench. They got wet almost fully; she dawdled close to him, looked to his eyes, smiled magnificently and enquired if she could cuddle him.

That was just a prelude; she held him closely, put her shoulder part of the sari on his head. She laughed, thanked the rain, slowly opened his shirt buttons and ran through her fingers on his hairy chest. She mumbled in his ears "I love the hair". She told him to unbutton her top and pressed his chest against her. There were none else, the rain picked up speed and it was becoming dark too. The thunder and lightning only spiced up their first encounter, leaving no space to think of anything else.

It was 8o'clock and though enervated, they walked to the car which was parked outside the garden. He dropped her at the Church Gate station, hugged each other a minute more and parted, both wishing for a faster Monday to show up. Thereafter, this kept happening every week and those were indeed very joyful days.

Jayawanti never had any intimate relations with any one before marriage or in the post marital 5 years as she was always in a traditional joint family which had several dos and don'ts. Her husband was an accountant later tried out to be a stock market player cum investor and spent lots of time in the evening with his own friends. He turned up late at home, did some talking with the rest of the large family members; then quickly caught up with his sleep after writing down or adding and subtracting figures in his diary. No child even after 5 years; 'it is her problem they said', it could be his, she thought. Nothing was certain yet, but they continued with the iroccasional doctor visits.

One day, she said to Hari "I would be happy if I get a child; that is all my wish now. I think Hari, we had some past connection, and otherwise we wouldn't have met or come so close. My heart says so". In the office, many sensed and talked about their friendship.

While this went on for more than a year, one day she informed that she and her family was shifting to Ahmedabad for good and as such she would be resigning from the job in the next 3 days.Though they felt deeply sad, those three evenings both spent most of their time together, being in the gardens, sipping coffee and eating candy. When sun dipped into the sea on the last day, they got closer, tarried united and wept for long time. It rained cats and dogs. She then clapped, laughed and hollered "I am pregnant".

****

IV   THE SPINSTER

Alpa came to the office around 4:30 p.m. and told the watchman that she needed to meet Mr. V.G. Sir and handover the office lease agreement copy. He asked her to sit at the reception room and went to the next cabin where the General Manager V.G. Krishna, his secretary and another staff seated. The rest of the office space was nicely done up for Director's cabin, Senior technical staff, Finance and

Accounts Manager and three lady staff members. V.G. Krishna was the face of the company who handled public relations, logistics, coordination with banks and financial institutions, administration, office staff selection and things like that. Everyone called him V.G. Sir and for the Director, he was just V.G or sometimes referred as 'Magician', for all troubles, issues and problems did finally go to V.G. who unraveled them.

The company was in technology business and the foreign educated elderly Director and other senior technical staff never got involved or knew anything of these sort of issues and governmental problems. Thus V G's hands were always full but he was highly touted and recognized by all.

Alpa smiled gorgeously and introduced herself as Alpa Shah and said the premises belonged to her mother Meenabai Sharad Shah since her father's death in a sudden road accident years ago. Her mother grew old and stopped going out anywhere except to temples or to attend exceptionally unavoidable family or social events. Hence, the 25-year-old Alpha held the 'Power of Attorney' for the dealings of all the properties and wealth related matters. She had graduated from Wilson College 5 years ago and her elder sister got married at the age of 29 and moved out to Virar (a western Mumbai suburb). The third and fourth are also girls, so she took up the responsibility of looking after all collection of rents from a couple of commercial premises, handling several disputes, court cases and so on.

Her late father Sharad Hasiklal Shah was a well-known tax consultant to many south Mumbai builders and thus he harnessed several premises in lieu of his services rendered. He was highly efficient, hardworking and made reasonably good fortune and name. He also made a small residential ground plus one floor building near Bhulabhai Desai Road, the ground commercial space was now let out to his company. The entire first floor had just three large flats for him and two of his brothers- Nikunjbhai and Bipinbhai who was partially deaf and dumb. The former was a college drop out.

Alpa kept talking garrulously, so V.G. alluded she could do the remaining next time since he had some work to get through and people almost started leaving the office as the work timing was 9 to 5:30. Alpa requested him to sit and bear with her a little more; she became emotional, and a few drops rolled out of her sublime eyes. He asked her to continue.

Her father got his brothers married, gave his flat also to the first brother who had two sons and   last brother had no children. Sharad Shah with five of his family members shifted to the new 3,500 sq. Flat at Walkeshwar; he was 45 years then and they were all small and her mother was a diabetic and asthmatic patient.

Ever since they shifted to the new house, the senior brother who had been a little willy nilly since earlier days started showing his displeasure about the new acquired house, though everything was made from the scratch by her father and there was nothing significant orinherited from their God loving father. To make things hard, he took his childless brother, his wife and relations on his side.

She sobbed and said, "in less than a year my father met with a big road accident and passed away at Ahmedabad in a very suspicious circumstance but then nothing came out of the investigations. I then decided to remain unmarried, dedicating myself for the support of my family. My elder sister was not good in studies and got dropped from the school; then arose several problems, discords, court issues all one after another, mostly crafted or aided by his own brothers – my uncles".

They got rid of her elder sister by getting her married to a petty shopkeeper from Virar. They were now at his mercy; he went out and collected all rents saying he was the one who looked after all affairs. Though their house was a large one, the cash flow remained a perennial problem and they had to visit virtually numerous times or make phone calls to receive the monthly agreed sum of Rupees thirty thousand to take care of domestic expenses. "So, sir I would request to pay this leased premises rent only to me and never to anyone of them". She got up, smiled graciously, thanked profusely and drove in her white Maruti van.

V.G. kept those agreement papers in a file in his cabin and noticed that everybody had left the office by then and it was past 6:30. He told the watchman to lock the office and left for home. On the way to his home, he thought about her pathetic situation despite good wealth, her issues and the way she aired them. Her English was quite good with good manners, grace, conviction, determination and boldness. She was very beautiful with well-rounded face, pointed nose and every time she smiled it resembled a full moon. She appeared very clear in her thoughts and words. She looked a bit chubby but that did not mitigate her beauty or look.

The second day evening she came again but that was around 6 when many in the office had left. She said she was passing through the road so just thought of enquiring if everything in the premises were fine. She handed over him again her contact number and requested him not to approach the people lived upstairs for anything. She then wondered if she could talk to him for a while as she found him to be very patient, kind, gentle and compassionate. She added that she felt relieved and felt so much happiness the previous evening.

While the first floor Nukunjbhai always greeted him whenever he met him in the premises and also occasionally peeped in saying whenever the office cheque was ready, he could come and collect same from him and pass it on immediately to them.

While this kept happening Alpa started coming to the office more often, sometimes 2-3 times a week under one guise or the other. The office people took note of this and sometime discussed among themselves that she was coming to spend time with him, taking some feeble excuses.

One evening she beseeched him to spend a little time with her and suggested he parked his car near Worli seaface, and she would follow him. When she insisted that she was seeing in him as a good brother or person and she had no one else to consult, take opinions from or confide, he agreed to spend a short while with her at the sea face.

She went on describing about the fineness of her father, how he had helped everyone but inspite of that his brothers ditched him and it was impossible for her to believe the road accident in which her father passed away was actually a mere accident and there should be something else to it. She and her family had been now put into several difficulties through disputes and litigations and his insistence on getting married as per his recommendations and proposal. She sat in his car a little later and sought his support and help whenever she needed. Her mother had no knowledge about anything as she was too weak and sick. The two younger sisters were very soft spoken saying all the time that they should be happy to depend on their uncle for whatever he was worth or else things would goeven more worse.

She also said that in other one or two properties, he went and collected rents offering some cash incentive to them, assuring he would take care of all problems and so on. He brought so much pressure on them to listen him and do things as per his wish and he would look after them. In reality he was a crook and very cunning; he could always convince the people through his impressive sugar talk.

Alpa kept calling VG on phone and visited at least 2-3 times every week if not more. She arrived about 5:30 p.m. or sometimes caught up with him on the way and spent time with him near the sea face; she changed over to his car or invited him to her's. She said she was getting maximum joy when she spent time with him and expressed gratitude for same. She sat very close to him, patted, then put her hands around him and once insisted on visiting his home, to meet his wife and parents.

She touched his parents' feet respectfully, told his wife she was so lucky to have a person like V.G.Sir who was extremely nice, gentle and helpful. She also briefly explained to them about her and her family members.

V.G. was not able to stop or avoid her continuous visits and physical intimacy. Once she invited him and wife for lunch to her house saying her mother and sisters were anxious to meet him and wife. They reached her house on a Sunday around 12 o'clock and took lunch and things like that. All of them were so nice saying Alpa keeps talking about V.G. sir and his superb nature, character and persona.

Later, one day she mentioned she wished to be his second wife and her mother and sisters were fully ok with that; she suggested he could come and stay with them once a week leaving all other days with his wife and parents. She pleaded that she would convince his wife and family members and she needed no financial support absolutely and their marriage would not be known to anyone outside the family and that would give her immense happiness and his sisters too would eventually get married; certainly she could not think of any other man in her life and she wanted a child through him.

V.G. explained to her the implications of that kind of fantacies and how this could create numerous complications for all in future. He opined that she could consider him as a good friend for moral support and she should think of getting married to someone if not immediately but in the near future. That day she cried incessantly, but he soothed her saying everything would fall in place slowly and he was available to her for any kind of help and free consultation.

In the following two years her two sisters got married and left Walkeshwar home leaving Alpa and her mother home. V.G. visited them once a while, hung on long hours, caring and contributing help in legal and other matters . Alpa remained unmarried forever.

****

V. VIRTUOUS WOMEN

Raghu got married at a very young age; he was going to be 28 years in the next 3 months. He completed his mechanical engineering and immediately got a campus placement; he was 21 years then. Raghu was the second son of his parents and the other one was senior to him by 5 years. He did his MBA after the engineering, immediately got a job and went to the US where he fell in love with an Australian colleague and never came home ever since. Raghu got married to a Keralite girl as per the wish of his parents so that was purely an arranged marriage. They lived at Prabha Devi in an old housing colony ground floor and there were a couple of buildings in that area.

Just one building, again in a ground floor flat which was closed for some years, as the owner family moved out to Goa, a new family had come to stay. They too were Goans – an old man and his wife with their daughter and granddaughter. They were confined to their home mostly except that every morning the child got picked up by a school van and the lady nicely dressed up, presumably left to her office by 9:30 in the morning.

That was how Raghu chanced to see her and at the very first time itself she presented a ducky smile to him. This happened when he took out his car and slowly passed her house to get onto the main road. He usually reached back by 7 o'clock and he saw her coming out of the house with her daughter, taking a short walk within the colony but returned quickly. Raghu after coming back from the office went for a walk in the nearby spacious garden surrounded by several small trees, plants and so on. Some played at one side, others did jogging, yoga or played cricket. The garden was very big but not the entire length and breadth of the landscape was well electrified. One could see many people sitting and relaxing, while some young couple paced fast or moved around.

Raghu's wife usually did her stroll along with her in-laws in the early evenings and also brought from market the fresh vegetables, eggs, fruits and other grocery items. Thereafter they watched television Programmes or serials in the leaving room. It was a small two bedroom house. For that matter, the entire buildings in that area looked more or less alike, with the ground plus three floors comprising one or two bedrooms with a kitchen.

When Raghu stepped out of his house for a walk, she was standing on her veranda.

She looked at him smilingly and he too smiled. This continued for the following two days. On the third day, he just signaled with his one hand and asked her to take a walk in the garden. "You move on and I will see you at the second left corner of the first entrance" She said. They met there and exchanged greetings. She was Rossi, worked for a Travel Agency some kilometers away at 'kemps corner' and her work time was 9:30 to 6:00, six days a week and her daughter studied in first standard in a Convent School. Her husband Rozario was in Saudi Arabia, working there on a three years contract and two years were already over. His elderly parents lived there, with she and her 5 year daughter Annie. "Annie is very beautiful like her mother" he commented. She giggled nodding her head. She then held his arm and said "thank you so much; you are very handsome, smart and generous." Her hands were warm. They conversed a little more and she said " I will go now and if it is ok, we could meet tomorrow again". She said bye and dissipated fast. Raghu jogged for another 20 minutes and left for home.

Next day, they met up at the same time. As he past walked her home, she smiled and slowly followed, keeping low pace to evade anyone looking. The garden corner they met was not very well lit and people generally moved around the garden or played quite at a distance from that corner. That way the space was very safe. for others hardly saw or looked at them. They stood very closely, touching each other and put their arms around. She whispered "maybe we had some connections, or it is the Lord's wish for things to be in this way. I feel enraptured when I am near you". She enquired about his job, wife, parents and other details in the meanwhile. They hugged each other so warmly and so profoundly; their hands moved all over. They were beginning to know each other well.

After some days, the love, longing and romance only got aggrandized. They cared and understood each other well. So one day she suggested "some Sunday should we go out somewhere and spend more time together, to Madh Island or somewhere? I could come out from home under the pretext of extra office work; would you?" Raghu replied "yes. He too thought there might be some earlier birth connections between them or it was God's will.

The next Sunday as planned they drove to Mudh island at about 9:30, Raghu picked her up from a nearby bus stop and reached the destination by 11:30. They rented out a room nearby, left their personal belongings there and went to swim for a while. They returned, had some beer, in the restaurant entered the room, switched on the fan and AC, sat on the bed and started chatting. The plan was to reach back home by 6:30 in the evening latest and as such it was imperative that they quit the place latest by 4:30 evening.

So there was only short space of time and they were naturally in great haste; the large mirror in the room reflected their emotions and intimacy which intensified their pleasure and exultation. They both said it many times. "We love and God helps".

Rossi was an orphan brought up in the nearby church and she absolutely had no knowledge of her parents and things like that. She studied at the same convent school and graduated from the nearby college in commerce. Her husband Rozario too was an adopted child of her in-laws. Whenever they visited the church, they saw many girls there. When she was about to finish her graduation the wedding proposal came from the church, and they did not have to consult anyone and their marriage got solemnized swiftly.

Rozario had finished his diploma in mechanical Engineering from 'Father Agnel Technical Institute' and was doing job in a private company, but he always wanted to go to a gulf country for better prospects. In a years' time they got a child who is now 5 years. He got a three year contract job in Saudi Arabia and his plan was to take his wife and daughter to Saudi in his next contract; its 2 years over.

Raghu and Rossi continued their relationship in this manner and Rozario came back on completion of his 3 years but luckily things worked out so well in about three months. That was the first time she, Annie and her husband Rozario came to say goodbye to Raghu and his family people. They sat for about 20 minutes in his home and spoke for a while. As they stood up to leave she sobbed and everyone thought she became emotional because they were leaving the locality. Tears rolled down from Raghu's eyes and he quickly blamed it for some dust particles entered his eyes. The pain, emotions and grief of two helpless soulmates merged in the air. Raghu said "we will meet one day or other" she said "we are going tomorrow morning" and informed that their house also would be vacated as the parents are planning to relocate to a small house in Goa once for all".

Many years had passed since that episode. Rozario's parents left for Goa. Raghu and Prema had no children; their parents too had passed away. Raghu and Prema spent their time mostly watching TV shows, visiting grocery stores, vegetable markets, temples and occasional short group trips and travels. He nurtured his hope and intuition that one day he would meet her again – she was so good. They sometime sat or strolled in the nearby gardens or visited the beach side of Shivaji Park area. Prema liked popcorn and Bhelpuri there. Raghu and Prema went to the beach on

Sunday, they both sat on the sand for a while as usual and Prema stepped out to look for some Bhelpuri. Raghu kept thinking about many things for that was in his nature for a very long time. He had read a lot and had substantial interest in variety of subjects like intuition, instinct, mysticism' supernatural elements, history, philosophy, life after death and like. We are God sent and then we go back to him some day. "But then why is this coming and going". He wondered.

He thought "We are happy sometimes, ask questions, go through sorrow, pleasure – both essential and devine. We live logically, illogically, ethically, unethically, truthfully and not so truthfully. We do right things, wrong things, leave with honesty, dishonesty, smile, cry, laugh. What do these things actually mean? What is the measure of logic or rational of anything. But human heart is so mysterious, inexplicable, it keeps many images within. If heart's cravings is not real what else is real?"

Ohh, my Raghu, how are you? Someone held hands and closed his eyes from behind. The hands were soft but warm and the grip was hard. He wondered "could this be the hands of Rossi?" "yes, Rossi, after a lapse of 3 decades" he swiftly took her hands, kissed on the palms, on her forehead and said "Prema is gone to get some Bhelpuri; why don't you sit down?" she kissed on his cheeks a few times and murmured. "Raghu, we are soul mates". She took a deep breath; her face resembled the moon at the sky which shied away in the clouds.

Prema returned with a plate of Bhelpuri and a small packet of popcorn. "Prema, could you recognize her?" said Rahu, she said "the face looks a little familiar but can't really figure out". Rossi began talking, "I was your neighbour sometime earlier moved away to a gulf country with husband Rozario and daughter. Rozario is no more. My daughter went to study in the US, married an Australian and not met ever since. Our parents passed away. Rozario died in a road accident some time ago. I live very close by alone; attend Naveena in the Mahim church every Wednesday. I have no friends, no relatives, just live alone; do not know how long, but now feel happy by meeting you and Raghu here. She took a long breath again. sobbed and then smiled – "should we stay together? You both staying with me sometime and me in return at your house?" She looked at Raghu and then Prema. Instantaneously, the three of them put their hands around and hugged. That lasted for a long time.

****

STORY GISTS

THE CRAVING HEARTS

The first story "Two Letters' is about the romantic entanglements of two women with a young Nval Officer at Tiupati during his Post Graduation in English Literature Examinations at shri Vnenkateshwara University and later receiving two different love letters from both, a long one and the other short.

The next story is about aman's' First love', one in the teenage period and at the other when he became an adult. Both occurred for a short time, then they got separated for 4-5 decades but his heart craved to see them once atleast and finally that did accomplish.

'The Innocuous girl' delve upon an intimate relationship of a young Executive with a married colleague Jayawanti. The fourth one speaks about the extra ordinary deep relationship of young Alpa with a senior General manager, who eventually wishing to be his second wife but remained a spinster throughout.

The last one is an angelic married woman gives her heart and soul to a married man but had a long break as she had to join her husband overseas for some three decades. She later findsand join him owing to changed circumstances and perhaps with God's wish.

******

Her Confessions

In 'Her Confessions' the Protagonist Meena a Senior MNC Manager, now in her late thirties chronologically, unveils her most intimate physical relationships and encounters from early childhood which ordinarily, none would brave, leave alone a young woman.

She opens up perhaps for her own set of reasons or pleasure, putting things threadbare, as she wants to catch up with and capture her past experiences looking through a prism.

She says it all – from what began from a close kinship, at home with cousin, and a neighbor during her primary school and high school days. She goes on with the first and subsequent love, even her strange and unusual intimate encounter with a young woman divorcee. It goes on and on - at her work places, during the course of office travel, after the birth of her children in her own house; closely about a dozen affairs in vivid settings. She has no grudges, accusations or complaints about anything or against any, including herself

******

THE IMPRESSIONS

The Novel appertain to different views and impressions the chief protagonist Prakash(nick name Unni) forms in his formative years four to fifteen as event occurs. At the age of four when he encountered 'Swami Krishanada' he wished to be a Saint. When an ardent LordKrishna devotee appeared he thought that person would become a rising star up the Sky and when he heard the story of hapless Potten (dumb, deaf and ugly) he assumed the man became like that because of his father was alcoholic and one should never touch that stuff. He revered the distant, old family connected Raghav mama for his selflessness and goodness.

The fifth chapter talks about his admiration for the old man Kunjhooti for his non dependence and making a living through his own way. Rangoon returned Moopan Mammad comes in the sixth chapter who created fear in every one's mind for his tough look and mistaken identity which he later realised and started liking him. And the character Thanikutty of seventh chapter appeared clever and mischievous .The next one is about his deep empathy for a particular neglected community of old Kerala and wanted to help them when he grew up. The next two chapters respectively are his analysis about one Krishna vaidyar who eventually became spiritual, and his own secondary school days.

The elderly woman Amminiamma who selflessly helped others earned his deep affection and sympathy which is discussed in Chapter XI. The following one is about one AppanNamboodiri and his childhood love for Sudhamma. The last chapter which is the XIII vividly goes into his School Vacation days that he spent with his uncle – a Naval Officer in Colaba, Mumbai, the joy and impressions which he treasured. The book will certainly make an excellent and rewarding experience which will linger in the mind for a long time.

*****

COL. SANDEEP

This delves into the two weeks Almora {spiritual city- Uttarakhand} tour that Col. Sandeep made along with his Navy commander friend in the aftermath of Covid – 19 in the month of November.

What transpires including his encounter with a Lady Army Officer and then what followed, is a fascinating read.

The second story 'Was She Insane?' is a question put by a 4 year old boy to his mother when a distant spinster cousin of her died early, after series of conventional medicines coupled with several rituals and pujas; throws light to many norms and practices of a bygone era.

'Thonu' is a brief sketch of an 80 year old women who visited once a while four wealthy village homes. Later events reveal an unusual and disturbing realities of her life.

'Kaki' speaks about a lone transgender – insignificant, hardly heard or seen around suddenly assumes importance, visibility and acclaims due to a single shocking incident in a small locality.

The last revolves around 'Kunjhaman' – a hapless man with a terrible childhood exerience but the life and the legacy of empathy that he left behind, would touch hearts and leave readers think.

******

7 STORIES

1. Black Cow – This happens in a Kerala Village home some 6 decades ago, when Appu was 3 years and his sister 5 years old. Father gets a Black cow with calf to pacify his wife's

complaint about the poor quality and delivery of the purchased milk, and then how the celebration goes around; also a few things that followed.

2. Three elopements goes into three love marriages by running away from home over a period of a decade or so in good old days of a place in Kerala, which until then or later never occurred in that manner.

3. Ustad is a story woven around two Navy men and a Naval base security guard in Goa in early seventies which presents the men, places and life style of then; this goes to the child hood love incident of the security guard and his fine character.

4. Gulmen is a special character, an old fashioned brass vessels cum lamps repairer who visited the village and camped in small houses and celebrated his life, though a loner

or a nomad. He brought joy to the surrounding people as well.

5. Gas Agency is a recent love story about two senior citizens of two different religions happens at the back drop of Corona ward in a Mumbai hospital and how it develops.

6. Gulikan and Parakutty are two demon deities of an old fashioned house that needed to be pleased occasionally by slightly unusual rituals; quite a few things are brought to the front for discussion.

7. The Flour Mill is yet again is about a very innocent and pure love that strangely takes place between two village teens which brought them happiness in those old fashioned times but only for a short while.

******

STORY OF RAVIKUMAR

During early part of 'Covid 19 lock out' leisure time this year, Ravikumar quite abruptly began reminiscing in the forenoon hours of 'Vishu' (Kerala new year day in mid April) a few random incidents but all occurred until he became about thirty nine years old and the last being his unplanned encounter with a 'Saint' at Rishkesh. These things are scripted in a perspicuous and stand alone fashion - worth giving it a read.

******

REVIEWS OF OTHER BOOKS

1.

Dr.PP Radhakrishnan, has a flair for writing. Recently he has released two books, '7 stories' and 'Story of Ravikumar' and are worth reading. His particular passion is in detailed description of every frame of story which he has not deliberately avoided to take the reader alongwith story line and he has well succeeded in this objective. Most of the seven stories well describe life in Indian cities and villages. 'Gas Agency' is indicative of plight of old people in many families in India. 'Ustad' well describes leisure life of Goa and likewise other stories. Each book is packed in some 90 to 100 pages to give an interesting reading to the reader.

Regards

SHRIRANG PRABHU

(Past District Governor, Rotary Dist. 3141, Mumbai)

2.

Story of Ravikumar

I must say that the author used the lockdown period very productively to produce a very good piece of literary work by penning 'The story of Ravikumar'. The language is lucid and the uncomplicated manner of narration makes the reading impulsive and captivating The author has deep insight into the dominant festivals of Kerala such as Vishu, NiraPoli etc. and has devoted a few pages to delve into them. Unfortunately, these days hardly anyone celebrates NiraPoli as the paddy fields, which were once used for cultivation of paddy, are fast becoming the hotbeds for construction of commercial and residential complexes. Nevertheless, it took me far down the memory lane and I was overwhelmed by a strong feeling of nostalgia when I wound up reading the book. Kudos to the author for bringing up glimpses of an ancient and venerable festival/ritual which is fast fading into oblivion in Kerala.

All in all, it's a good book to read and I wish the author all the very best and urge him to take up writing in a more serious manner.

JayarajMenon, Belapur

3.

I immensely enjoyed reading 'The Story of Ravikumar' and there was never a dull moment. Author has very beautifully described several incidents which Ravikumar encountered during his early phase of life - be his romance, his stint with corporate life, train journey, trip to Rishikesh.

The Village of the bygone era, Panchayat office arrangements to light up two pole kerosine lamps through employee Kumaran who walked every evening with an old fashioned bamboo ladder on his shoulder, oil can in hand and lighting up the lamp is a visual that will never fade away from the mind. The description of several traditional festivals like Vishu, Nirapoli, temple festivals and so on so forth are truly fascinating. I wish the Author all the very best and he comes up with more such interesting books.

- Nayana, Cochin

4.

My review of the book '7 Stories'
The seven stories that the author has narrated in his book titled '7 Stories' made interesting reading. The story on the 'Black Cow' touched an emotional chord in my heart, for such incidents were commonplace for any child during childhood. The author has successfully made a deep imprint of Appu's excitement in the readers' mind. Every household is certain to have had an Appu in its midst in the good old days and the story of the 'Black Cow' brought back vivid memories of my long-lost childhood as well.

The other stories such as Gulmen, The Flour Mill and Gulikan&Parakutty were no less captivating. In short, the seven stories are like the seven hues of the rainbow and are as resplendent. I must say that I read the book twice over as some of the stories; I felt, had some strange connotations with my childhood life. Thanks to the author for taking me down the memory lane at least for a casual stroll of sorts.

JayarajMenon
Belapur.

5.

7 Stories' another book by the author of 'Story of Ravikumar' is truly fascinating. Enjoyed reading all the seven, equally relished by grand-daughter too. The first story 'Black Cow' evoked child hood memories and Appu's excitement would touch hearts. Though the story of 'Three Elopements' were uncommon then, gossips amongst women in temple bathing ponds about such things were there, once a while.

The story of 'Ustad' brings to the forefront' the life style of Goa then, while 'Gulmen' story captures a special village character who can be easily visualised.

'Gas Agency' is quite a heart touching love story of Gopan and Fathima happens in a Mumbai hospital Corona Ward but with a painful end, and 'The Flour Mill' is an innocent short lived romance story of two teenagers yet again of two different communities

'Guligan&Parakutty are about two evil gods of a bygone era in a Kerala village and half yearly rituals of pleasing them. The stories did strike a chord with me and the author is indeed a good story teller. I wish him the very best. –

 Nayana, Cochin

6.

Read "7 Short Stories" today. A Pleasure of being transported to Gods Own Country through your lines, incidentally my association with Kerala started in 1980's with my work at Munnar Tea Gardens and lasted for three and a half decades. Thank you PP for bringing fond memories back.Congratulations and wish you the best in you new endeavour

S Sengupta,
Mumbai

7.

Reading the book inadvertently gets you involved in many a Malayaleefestival ,Vishu being of utmost importance and NiraPoli as mentioned above being the other. Well, you literally get a feeling that you are part of the very Malayalee family of Ravi celebrating the festivals.

The book brings forth a Canvas of the happenings in old time Kerala, what with the green Paddy fields, swaying palms, serene back waters, kerosene lamp lit thatched huts and the undulating movements of the house boats – after all it's not for nothing that Kerala is called "Gods own Country ". The descriptions of the people, the women folk, their attire and of course the cook -one Mr.Kuttan Nair and the ever-delicious boiled banana or the fried banana chips – all takes you back in times.
The book is a good read in Covid times particularly if you wish to wash the Corona Blues / depression. The book has all the makings to be converted into a full range Motion Picture and considering the immense popularity in the learned, discerning people I see the making of a best seller.

The end comes in the form of an unplanned encounter with a saint at the holy Rishikesh a literary climax in itself. The book could have been easily paraphrased as an Autobiography of the writer for one sees the author reliving himself as every page unfolds.

A must read

Wish him well! Just to add the Author Dr PP Radhakrishnan is good friend of mine, a neighbor and a very good human being.

Rtn. Dr.Anoop Kumar Gupta. Consultant Gynaecologist. MD,

DGO, FCPS, DNB.Mumbai.

8.

Dr PP Radhakrishnan's book "Col Sandeep" is a beautiful story from times of the pandemic. His style is evocative of typical Indian society, with a flair for telling a story in the simplest language. This makes his storytelling relatable to the Indian masses and readers like myself. It was a pleasure hosting and meeting him at Deodar Homestay, Almora.

ShekharLakhchaura

Almora

9.

Review by: Shrirang Prabhu

Dr. PP Radhakrishnan

Rotarian P.P Radhakrishnan is known for his very useful booklets on Rotary subjects. Lately he also ventured into non Rotary subjects with interesting stories.

His recent book 'COL SANDEEP' mostly sketches village life except first chapter on Col. Sandeep. Author ably describes various shades of human life and brings to readers flavor of different village personalities. In 'COL SANDEEP' story, author describes well army environment in Navy Nagar, Mumbai and equally well spiritual surroundings of Almora. Story ends on a very refreshing note. In contrast, the second story 'Was She Insane' ends up with heart touching sad end of a girl , victim of age old rituals and practices. In next chapter 'Thonu' author interestingly depicts how the lady was dressed up traditionally with " Dhoti" and "Vesti", Usual dress for many poor lady and the habit of preparing and sharing "Pan" (Beetle Leaves)with others; general in village households. Chapter 'Kaki' deals with an insignificant, manly lady, in fact a transgender, how comes to prominence when she punishes the village miscreant. Author also writes about how small amount of ganja and alcohol was not forbidden in poor households particularly during festivities of deities. Chapter on 'Kunjhaman' ends up with ceremonial death of poor lonely man having a big heart, how he donated all his meagre lifesaving to poor school children. Kindness does not require big resources. To conclude, stories are mostly about people from villages from south India and truly makes a good reading to know better life there particularly in olden days.

Shrirang Prabhu
Past Governor Rotary Dist. 3141.

10.

Story of Ravikumar

Book is so calm and positive filled with real life experiences of this Author. It depicts Author's compassion and excellence towards story telling. Had a great time reading this story and was so intriguing. Really loved how the story was to the point and elements were accurately phrased to create more interest. Give it a try and you guys will not regret a second. Kudos to the Author!

Priyanka, Arizona.

11.
To conclude, stories are mostly about people from villages from south India and truly makes a good reading to know better life there particularly in olden days.

Shrirang Prabhu

Past Governor Rotary Dist. 3141.which leave a lasting imprint in the minds of the readers.

The story of Col. Sandeep is about a visit by him with his friend Commander Madhav during the days of Covid 19 to Almora where they meet Bina who tells them about her friend Bhagya who was in the army in Mumbai. The story has an element of suspense which keeps the readers intrigued till the end. The author has deftly woven the story, interspersing a brief account of the pristine landscape of the holy place Almora as well as a throwback to the romance of Col. Sandeep and Bhagya, during the days of their courtship in Mumbai.

The second story 'Was she insane' narrates the harrowing tale of Banu who's a spinster and lived the life of a recluse. She develops a mysterious disease and is placed in confinement. Banu eventually dies in fetters and the tale of her misery has been eloquently described by the author in his inimitable manner.

The third story of 'Thonu' is about an old character,who used to frequent a few select houses in the village. Little Chandra had a fondness for Thonu and when she did not visit the village for some days little Chandra, her mother and a few others set out to Thonu's house only to find that 'Thonu' had died in her shanty in her nondescript village a few days back. The author has successfully narrated the empathy and grief of little Chandra in a subtle manner.

The fourth story is about 'Kaki' the transgender. She is a bold character and provided protection to Charu and her two good-looking daughters from the evil gazes of the village louts. The last one is the story of Kunjhaman who toils hard by doingodd jobs to make a living in a village that has adopted him into its fold. The hardship that Kunjhaman endures during the course of his life has been narrated by the author in a heart-rending manner. I think the author, with each book, has raised the bar by several notches which makes reading of the stories a gripping and captivating experience.

JayarajMenon, Belapur

12.

My review of each of Dr. P.P. Radhakrishnan's three books comes together as it contains many common threads. Above all, the simplicity of the language and yet its literary value is excellent. The fragrance of village soil comes from their stories and novels. The unfamiliar customs of Kerala, the atmosphere there, made a Marathi person like me happy to learn new things. His writing style is very pictorial. Here I will make special mention of Thonu's personality portrayal.

The elaboration of her nose ring, her brown sheen to clothing is so beautiful and detailed that it looks like she is standing in front of us alive. The reader becomes acquainted with the small incidents in Ravikumar's life. And it was funny to read the stories of people who ran away and got married in those times when love marriage was not very common and its effect on the village. Keep writing.

VarshaKolhatkar

13.

Dr. PP Radhakrishnan's book Col. Sandeep is an excellent collection of stories, these stories are such that each character seems to come alive and you feel the things happening around you. The emotions of the characters have been brought out in such manner that you relate yourself with the stories.

The emotions of an army officer, the village life, hardships and the little things that being happiness are so well documented that you can't stop yourself in reading the book entirely at a stretch.

Dr.Radhakrishnan in his literary work included common people and their experiences in life, this shows his deep understanding of the social structure and his feelings about relationships.

His works I understand from other reviews are par excellence and has created curiosity to read all his books too.

I wish him good luck for his future literary creations.

VinodChaube

Banking Professional

14.

My review for your book - Story of Ravikumar!

The book "Story of Ravikumar" is collection of thoughts which depicts a person in his various emotions. The story about one's life where one experiences various situations in life. The construct of the story divide into various chapters gives you flavor of a village life, the daily routines, festivals, professional life, struggle, success, learning, touch of romance and brings you towards faith and spirituality.

Dr. PP Radhakrishnan has in the time at his disposal during pandemic lockdown has penned his thought very passionately.

It is joy to read his book, they are short and written with such simplicity that you relate yourself with characters and the story.

My best wishes to Dr.Radhakrishnan for his new literary creations.

Vinod Chaube

Banking Professional

15.

In PP Radhakrishnan's debut novella, the protagonist Ravikumar comes alive. A Malayalee, all of 39 years reminisces on his life in the difficult and confusing time of Corona. His mind is like a TV serial on a fast rewind. Discrete episodes flash by in short bytes.Pictures in a loose-leaf book format with no apparent order of continuity, Ravikumar moves through his life from a village in Palghat to an ashram in Haridwar and the journey is captured in short snippets of soliloque.You can feel the pleasant nostalgia under current in the reminiscences of the protogonist. Dr.Radhakrishnan's novella- Story of Ravikumar- is an ideal corona Read. It is racy. It is neither heavy on prose nor too light and chippy. Ravikumar's reflection on his life will let in a refreshing breath with its exact mix of elements to lift you up in his dreary lockdown.

NARAYAN SHARMA, MUMBAI

16.

7 Stories

The stories narrated in the book are stories of a village life. How a family is so
eagerly awaits a cow that was expected to address the concerns of family, the arrival and its being at home was celebrated.

The chapters in the book also depict the instances of unheard-of elopement by few lover couples who married despite resistance from family. Ordinary people such as Ustad a Sentry at the Naval base too have a life of his own which author has highlighted well.

The author has also included the unfortunate times of pandemic in the story and a love story developing in such hard time.

In stories delicate moments of teenage love has been highlighted at the same time the demon deity worships practiced in villages is also covered.

Overall the book keeps you engaged, the stories take you through different eras of village and modern life.

Reading this book is a pleasure.

Vinod Chaube

Banking Professional

17.

Col.Sandeep.

The author of this book has proved once again that he is a good story teller. He describes the life of people in the olden villages very vividly.

Apart from the title story of Col. Sandeep which is about two former Defence officers' sudden trip to Almora city in Uttarakhand during Covid time where they chanced to meet a serving defense lady officer and an extremely interesting story develops there after. 'Was She insane' is a heart breaking story of aspinster who gets mentally deranged and about her pathetic plight of life and death. Fourth story 'Kaki' is about an insignificant transgender who suddenly attains glory and praise owing to her handling a peculiar incident with extreme valour and impact. 'Kunjhaman' the fifth story is about a haplessman who had a shocking and horrifying childhood but yet his thoughts and concern for poor kids was astonishingly noble but that aspect came to be known only after his death which made the village people weep. Indeed an heart rending story. I now look forward to his next novel 'The Impressions'

Nayana, Cochin

18.

Dr. PP Radhakrishnan, has a flair for writing. Recently he has released two books, '7 stories' and 'Story of Ravikumar' and are worth reading . His particular passion is in detailed description of every frame of story which he has not deliberately avoided to take the reader alongwith story line and he has well succeeded in this objective . Most of the seven stories well describe life in Indian cities and villages . 'Gas Agency' is indicative of plight of old people in many families in India . 'Ustad' well describes leisure life of Goa and likewise other stories. Story of Ravikumar more intensly written narrating Raj kumar's childhood of olden days in a sleepy village of Kerala to his encounter with a Sadhu at Rishikesh in between, his Corporate stints sprinkled with some tender love encounters which usually happen when one grows up. Although PP has said it is a fiction story, every reason to believe that it is someone's life story worth reading.

Regards

SHRIRANG PRABHU

(Past District Governor, Rotary Dist. 3141, Mumbai).

19.

Review of ' The Impressions'

It gave immense joy to read this book. The author has described the life of the village folks in a simple and beautiful manner. The description on how they go about their daily life and affairs, the various stages of emotions the main character Unni underwent from the age of 4 to 15 forming his own impressions and the last being his romantic encounter during his vacation with a girl in Mumbai. Like his earlier fiction books, Story of RaviKumar, 7 Stories, Col. Sandeep, in this too the author has displayed vivid sense of storytelling which leaves a lasting impression on the readers' mind. The book is recommended for all ages. - Nayna, Cochin

20.

My words on some of books from Rtn. Dr.PP Radhakrishnan

I chanced to read some of the books authored by Rtn. Dr.PP Radhakrishnan recently while travelling.

The contents are very descriptive and the narrative is lucid. The author has virtually presented geographical details of the regions of Uttarakhand, Almora and

Kumaon in addition to important temples in the hill state. Col Sandeep finding a soulmate is a welcome decision.

In one of the stories, Chandra was very attached to Thonu and could not emotionally control her demise. In another story, little Balan was very fond of BhanuChechi simply unable to accept her cruel and gruesome death due to aggressive mental health. He simply asked his mother: Was she insane?

Well written narrative arousing curiosity throughout! In his first novella The Story of Ravikumar, the author has beautifully reflected on the traditional times of Kerala particularly, the people, culture, tradition, festivals, (apart from Vishu that has retained its sheen even today), romance folklores, religious diversity custom, temples, in comparison to the life styles in metro cities.

This 100 plus page novel compels to read in one sitting!

21.

The Impressions, another interesting book which cannot be missed, speaks about the chief protagonist Prakash – Unni makes his own assessments from his childhood to adulthood as the event unfolds…like at the age of 4 he wishes to be a saint when he meets one. In another instance, his deep empathy for a particular neglected community of old Kerala and wanted to help them when he grew up. In the last one where he spends his school vacation with his Naval officer uncle in Mumbai he develops a deep liking for a girl in the Naval quarters.

The 7 Stories (there are 7 heart touching short stories) are a blend of traditional and folk narration deftly weaved for an interesting read in the modern digital age.
They gently remind the present generations of the rich culture of the past, archived for posterity!

S Sampat Kumar – Navi Mumbai

22.

REVIEW OF BOOK " THE IMPRESSIONS"
The author's ability to intricately weave together a variety of themes and plotlines within the collection of stories is truly remarkable. The narrative seamlessly transitions from one tale to the next, allowing the reader to become fully immersed in the rich tapestry of the book. With each story, the protagonist Prakash gains a deeper understanding of the world around him, as well as his own inner self.
The character development throughout the book is a testament to the author's skill in creating multifaceted and relatable characters. From Krishnanada's quest for spiritual enlightenment stretching to various other

characters of the string of stories, each character brings a unique perspective to the overarching themes of love, loss, and spirituality.

Further more, the author's use of vivid and evocative language creates a rich sensory experience for the reader, bringing each scene to life with vibrant detail. The description of Prakash's vacation days in Mumbai, in particular, is breathtakingly beautiful, capturing both the excitement and melancholy of young love. Finally the heart-wrenching scene in which Prakash and Amba bid farewell to each other at the railway station is told with such raw emotion that it brought tears to my eyes, but the tender embrace that Prakash received from Amba ultimately helped me to compose myself.

Overall, the author's masterful storytelling and richly developed characters make this collection of stories a truly captivating read, leaving a lasting impact on the reader long after the final page has been turned.

JayarajMenon
CBD Belapur

Dr. PP Radhakrishnan

PUBLISHING DETAILS

CONTACT US FOR   PUBLISHING YOUR OWN BOOK

MAIL I'D –
aswanisomya1710@gamil.com

somyaaswani@gmail.com

CONTACT NUMBER - +91 8698468485

www.ingramcontent.com/pod-product-compliance
Lightning Source LLC
Chambersburg PA
CBHW040810120726
48005CB00012B/1370